For Sir Aidan of No Pants

Hi!

When I was about seven years old, my mother took me to our town's public library. There was a children's section, and that's where we went. I looked at the books lining the walls and after a brief time saw "One Fish Two Fish Red Fish Blue Fish" by Dr. Seuss. I could not believe it.

Over 50 years later, I can still remember the feeling of taking that book from the shelf and opening it. I can still smell the room and the scent of the pages as I started reading it. The idea that I could take it home with me was beyond amazing; at that moment it was the greatest thing that could have happened to me.

My mother used to read poems to me from an anthology she had, later I read them myself. The Animal Fair, Little Orphan Annie and others. I committed them to memory and would recite them whenever the opportunity arose.

Now, at 64, I am watching my grandson during the day and he loves being read to. He is especially fond of "Hop on Pop" and, as you might guess, "One Fish Two Fish". I was inspired to write some poems.

The poems in this book come from an idea that was stuck in my mind for months; the idea that there are things that start outside of something, go inside, and then come back outside. Each of the poems explores a variation on that theme. I hope you enjoy them!

Contents

A Cow Eats Grass All Day

Grass comes from a tiny seed
Down in the earth, it feels the need
To pop and push and strain and grow
Above the dirt, into the glow.

Alas, and after all of that,
A cow comes by named Butterfat
And bites the grass across the stalk
Then moves ahead in a slow, slow walk
To bite more grasses from their roots
Without a care, without a hoot.

The stalks of grass are now inside
Our Butterfat and down they slide
From mouth to stomachs, then they go
For more digestion down below.

They're pushed and squashed all in a group,
They lump and clump and turn to poop
Inside her butt, where it resides,
Until she pushes it outside.

The farmer takes the bovine waste
And scatters it across the place
To fertilize the ground, you know
And then grass seed the farmer sows
In fields, where Butterfat will eat
The new green grass grows tall and sweet.

Sir Aidan of Pants

There once was a boy named Sir Aidan of Pants,
Who wanted to go to the Middle School dance.
Sir Aidan he knew that the tunes would be poppin',
because of that music the place would be hoppin'.

Sir Aidan of Pants got his name from his slacks;
It was mainly because that of slacks he had stacks,
In colors and styles and textures and patterns,
He even had ones that had patterns of Saturns.

He picked out the pair that he liked just the best,
He lifted them, looked to make sure they were pressed.
He sat on his bed and he lifted his knee,
And put his foot into the pants by degree.

His foot through the length of the pants it did glide,
He tugged and he pulled till his leg was inside.
The other leg slid down the same as the first,
Only then did he realize his pants were reversed.

Sir Aidan took note and he cried, "What a sight!"
He turned them around and he put them on right.
Then Aidan, Sir Aidan, the pasha of pants,
Was ready to go to the middle school dance.

Washing Machines and Dryers

We wear clothes to keep us warm,
They can protect our skin from harm.
But after days or weeks of wear,
They need some cleaning and some care.

Into a hamper go the clothes
Until their odor finds our nose,
Then the need is mighty urgent
To wash them with a strong detergent.

Wet clothes do no one any good,
And drying them is understood
To be a challenge needing boldness
So you won't feel the damp and coldness.

One day when you're old enough
To take the clothes and other stuff
And lift the lid of that machine,
You'll put them in and get them clean.

And then you'll have a choice to make:
To hang them on a line to bake,
Or you might think that they require
Some time to roll inside a dryer.

Either way they lack the dirt
That once was on your pants and shirt.
Just fold them up, put them away
Next week you'll wear them out to play.

Teeth

A toothbrush is a vital tool,
To keep you looking mighty cool.
With your friends or at your school,
You brush your teeth, you aren't a fool.

Your toothbrush needs some help of course,
The toothpaste tube is just the source,
To help the brush scrub all your teeth,
The ones on top and those beneath.

Toothpaste does another job
When changing from a little blob,
It flows around your mouth like jelly,
And stops your breath from being smelly.

And when your teeth are all cleaned up,
You'll rinse your mouth, you'll use a cup,
You'll wash the toothbrush like a boss,
And won't forget the dental floss.

Visitors

Sometimes when you are home alone
You might go and pick up a phone,
To call your friend and ask and see
If they would like your company.

You leave your house and walk or ride
To your friend's door, then go inside,
Where they might offer you a hug
And sarsaparilla in a mug.

You might play tag, you might hang out,
Hear some music, dance and shout!
The mother of your friend might say,
"There's nothing quiet you could play?"

Then some time later you will know
Back to your home you have to go;
You hug your friend and say goodbye,
And step outside and home you fly.

Vacuums

Wherever you live, in a house, shack or shed,
Your dwelling has sides and a roof overhead.
Below it has wood floors or carpet or concrete,
Upon which you walk in your shoes or bare feet.

Your floor will get dirty from many a thing,
From crumbles of cookies to small bits of string,
From cat hair to dog hair to parakeet feathers,
And mud from your shoes and from big get-togethers.

The floor or the carpet get covered with gunk,
The stairs and the hallway, the room where you bunk,
It has to be cleaned 'cause if you let it go,
You never know what kind of fungus might grow.

To tidy the mess, I just might recommend
(and if you feel doubtful, then go ask a friend),
Take a ride to the store and go into the back room,
From a row on the wall you can pick out a vacuum.

The vacuum and parts they will come in a pack,
When you get it home, and if you have the knack,
You will put it together, the parts and the plug,
And now you are ready to vacuum your rug.

With a hum and a thrum and a vrumm-vrumm-vrumm-vrumm,
The vacuum works hard to pick up every crumb,
Every cat hair and feather and mud that's been dried,
All the bits that were down there get sucked up inside.

And then when the vacuum is all filled with gluck,
You will need a good way to get rid of that muck.
You'll carry the vacuum around to the back,
You'll let the dirt out of it, into a sack.

Your floors and your rugs are now clean and they're neat,
You've made each one spotless, you'll feel so upbeat.
And as for the dirt and the dust and the mess,
It all will end up in a landfill, I guess.

Boats

Thea Bean went on a trip,
Across the water, took a ship,
But Thea'd never been to sea,
And didn't know how it would be.

The morning came to get on board
So Thea, with a mighty hoard,
Lined up to get onto the boat
That would to small Nantucket float.

Thea Bean stood at the rail,
The horns blew and the ship set sail.
The captain steered clear of the shore,
And sailed just as she'd done before.

The ship, instead of being steady
Began to rock and roll already,
They weren't even on the ocean
When Thea felt a rolling motion.

Thea Bean became uneasy,
In her belly she was queasy,
She said she had to take a seat,
She found a chair, got off her feet.

Thea then began to change,
Her color, it began to range
From yellowish to olive green,
She knew she needed Dramamine.

When finally she turned to gray,
Thea Bean was heard to say,
"Someone needs to get a bucket
I'll never make it to Nantucket!"

Thea staggered to the side,
Leaned over, and abruptly cried,
"Look out below you sharks and fluke
Cause here it comes, I have to puke!"

Her breakfast fell into the brine,
No fish were harmed, which was just fine;
Then Thea felt a little better,
She sat back down, put on her sweater.

When finally the boat was docked,
Straight down the gangplank Thea walked.
She said to someone just ahead,
"I think next time I'll swim instead."

Raoul Ruiz

Raoul Ruiz had many a friend,
Some were just beyond the bend,
Others Raoul rode to see,
The rest he flew to meet for tea.

Raoul Ruiz had friends in France
and Spain that did the tango dance.
In Egypt, Benin and Japan
Where they invented folding fans.

His pals grew up in Germany
Where bratwurst was a guarantee.
In Paraguay and Singapore,
And even at the Jersey shore.

Raoul liked to keep in touch
Through talking on the phone and such,
But how he liked to reach out best
Was through the letters he addressed.

See, Raoul was a writing beast,
He wrote five notes a day, at least
To tell his friends how he was doing,
And ask them what they were pursuing.

When at last he stopped his pen
He'd read the letters over again
To make sure he used proper words,
Then folded them in even thirds.

Inside their envelopes they went,
And then into the mailbox sent,
From there the letters were dispatched
And went to whom the address matched.

When the letters were delivered,
Each friend quaked and each one quivered.
All said, "I can't wait to see
What Raoul Ruiz wrote to me!"

Each one was opened with commotion,
His friends were filled with big emotion,
They took the letters from their pouch
And went to read them on the couch.

Then once the letters all were read,
The readers from their couches sped
To grab a paper and a pen,
And write back to Raoul again.

Reading

When you open up a book
And then within you take a look,
Another world might there await,
Upon which you can cogitate.

If you can read, it's yay! for you,
And if you can't you'll just make do
Till one who can comes right along,
And reads to you both loud and long.

Whether you read by yourself
Or are read to by someone else,
The words go in your eyes or ears
And live within your brain for years.

It might have been a poem you heard
That you remember word for word,
You'll be so proud you will repeat
That poem to every one you meet.

Or maybe you will read a book
That has ideas on how to cook,
You choose one recipe to make:
A steak, a cake, a cookie bake.

Then all your friends can come and eat,
What you have made, salty or sweet,
You tell them that you made the food,
Thanks to the recipe you viewed.

Yes reading books can bring in notions
That make you think and feel emotions,
Ideas that let you change your mind
About the world and what you'll find.

Cats

Some people share their home with cats,
Some calicos, some white and blacks,
Some striped and tans, some browny-grays,
Some fluffy fat, some skinny strays.

There are three schools of thought, you see
That differ by a vast degree
On whether cats should live inside,
Go in and out, or stay outside.

This thinking happens by the cats
And those that share their habitats.

The problem comes, and all agree
When cat and human fail to be
In accord on which is better,
And how much time to spend together.

Some people like their cats inside
And there are cats that like to hide
Behind the door, under the bed
Where it is warm and they are fed.

But there are cats that want to roam
Around the block and far from home;
Inside the house they set their feet
Solely when they want to eat.

And finally, there are felines
That only want to make bee-lines
Away from children, moms and houses
And live outside and catch some mouses.

Ants

Ants are common,
They can be found
In groups above
Or under the ground.

They're yellow or orange,
White, blue or red,
Black, green or purple
Or rainbow instead.

Ants eat most everything:
Berries and crumbs,
Other bugs, birthday cake,
Peanuts and plums.

Ants leave the anthill
To go gather food,
Then haul it inside
To nourish their brood.

Tiny but mighty
Ants shoulder great weights –
One ant can lift
Up to 50 nest-mates!

They carry their babies
With ultimate care
When danger is coming
Or if there's a scare.

Ants care for each other:
If one has a gash,
A nurse ant will tend to it
Quick as a flash.

Tiny and colorful,
Caring and strong,
The ants in a colony
All get along.

Bath Time

In the morning or at night,
It could be noon if the time is right,
If you are dirty or if you stink
You might land in the kitchen sink.

Or maybe in the bathroom tub
You'll give yourself a scrub-a-dub,
But first you have to climb inside,
Into some water you may slide.

The water could be bubble-filled,
A place to play, you could be thrilled.
It might be cold or warm or hot,
Depending on your bathing spot

Inside a tub, inside a crock,
A lake, a pool, the sea, a loch,
You get into the water then
You wash and get back out again.

And when you leave the bathing trough,
You'll need a dry, dry, drying cloth
To wipe the water from your body
So you don't end up pruny-soggy.

Outside the tub,
Inside to scrub,
Outside to dry,
And bath, good-bye!

Thea Bean

Thea Bean was ten years old
When she caught a common cold.
She sneezed and coughed and blew her nose,
It ran just like a fire hose

The reason Thea Bean was ailing
Was all due to a subway railing.
A person that she did not know
held that rail an hour ago.

That someone, he was feeling poorly,
And sneezed into the air, which surely
Spread germs into the entryway,
Due to his sneezey-wheezy spray.

Some of the viral germs they landed
On the rail where they were stranded,
Till Thea Bean came down that stair
Holding to the rail with care.

All the germs they then elected
To make sure Thea was infected;
They stuck onto her pinkish palms,
Those tiny little germy bombs.

Later Thea rubbed her eyes,
Wow! She was in for some surprise
Cause all the germs upon her hand
In both her eyes did surely land.

From there they made her body sick,
But Thea knew a little trick
To block the spray that spreads disease,
So those around could feel at ease.

Thea knew that when she coughed,
The germs would likely go aloft
And land on someone's face and hair,
And make them ail and make them swear.

As Thea's cough or sneeze came out,
She moved her elbow to her snout.
From there the germs could not be spread,
They'd stay there till they're good and dead.

Drinking Water

When you're thirsty and want a drink,
You head straight to the kitchen sink
And pour the water, Just as you oughta
Into a cup, and drink it up.

The water comes out of the tap,
Or from a bottle with a cap,
Or maybe it was in a flask,
Or flowed out of a wooden cask.

Whichever way, the water flows
From spout to cup and on it goes,
From cup to lip to in your mouth,
You swallow and it slips due south.

It spills into your stomach, then
It sloshes to your intestine.
Intestines suck some water out
To help your blood and skin, no doubt.

Some of the water your body uses,
And some of it, it just refuses.
What happens to the extra drink?
Your kidneys get it in a blink.

Kidneys are bean-shaped body parts
Astride our spines, below our hearts
They filter all of what you drank,
Sending extra to your holding tank.

That holding tank is called your bladder,
It's made of muscle and other matter.

The liquid's stored till right on cue
You know you need to find the loo,
And after that, the next you see,
The stuff you drank comes out as pee.

Flying Fish

The sea is vast and deep and wide,
With lots of wiggly things inside,
Like marlin, eels and octopi,
Smelts and whales and fish that fly.

The sea is home to many creatures,
Because they have specific features:
Fish have gills and scales and fins,
Instead of lungs and hands and skin.

There is a fish within the ocean,
That moves with a peculiar motion.
The flying fish has long, long fins,
And uses them to catch the winds.

They don't have feathers like the fowl,
Who soar on wings, like snowy owls,
A flying fish will use its tail
To launch itself into a gale.

It glides and skims above the waves,
This fish is strong, this fish is brave,
This fish can sail a quarter mile,
In special flying fish-like style.

The flying fish must take good care,
To make sure when they're in mid-air,
That back into the sea they dip,
And do not land on decks of ships.

Breathing

Breathing, which you do automatically,
Is a problem if it's done erratically.
Breathing keeps us all alive,
Allows our bodies to survive.

The air around us is composed
Of oxygen which is supposed
To mix with sugar in each cell,
And keep them working very well.

How does the oxygen get inside
To cells that in our selves reside?
It comes in through our mouth or nose,
And down into our lungs it goes.

The lungs are like two pink balloons,
With wrinkles like your grandma's prunes.
When we breathe in they fill with air,
They swell and stretch, they're quite a pair.

To do their work the lungs rely
On pockets called alveoli.
The oxygen glides into these pockets,
Then jets into our blood like rockets.

From lung to blood and then it flows,
Right to the cells from head to toes
Where then with sugar it is tied,
Creating carbon dioxide.

Carbon dioxide is a gas
That quickly from the cells must pass;
If it does not and it increased
Your cells would then become deceased.

But worry not, your body senses
That CO2 has consequences.
Its seeps from cell to blood in traces,
And right back to the lungs it races

When we breathe out, the gas is sent
Where all the other exhales went,
Outside your lungs, outside your nose,
To Acapulco, I suppose.

Lucy

On the day the pigs were born,
The weather it was nice and warm.
Seven of the pigs were pink,
And three of them were black as ink,
But most surprising of the crew
Was Lucy, who was big and blue.

Now no one knows how Lucy came
To have a large and bluish frame;
She didn't seem to give a fig,
And neither did the other pigs
Who ran and played inside their sty,
Underneath the blue clear sky.

Our Lucy had a heart that yearned
To see the world; her heart, it burned,
To leave the comfort of her home,
And see the world, to range and roam
Across the sea, across the land,
And join a barnyard punk rock band.

One night when all the pigs were sleeping,
Lucy, to the fence went creeping;
She got there and she dug and squeezed
Till underneath the fence she eased,
When suddenly she heard a sound,
And toward that sound her way she wound.

It came from near the chicken coop,
And there she saw a biggish group,
The animals had come together
To hear the farm band "Chicken Feather".
The band were critters rocking punk,
A bit of blues, a bit of funk.

A rooster played the lead guitar,
The greatest shredder near or far;
The local draft horse played the bass,
He kept the beat, he set the pace;
Elvira goat she hit the drum,
The audience was overcome.

Lucy pig just stood in awe
While hearing what she heard and saw,
When suddenly she grasped the fact,
There was no singer in the act.
So when the band was on their break,
She went backstage, her claim to stake.

When they saw her, big and blue,
They knew just what they had to do,
They asked her if she'd join their crew,
To which she said, "Oh yes, thank you!"
She knew that she would fit just fine,
A grunting, snorting punk-rock swine.

The band kept playing till near dawn,
When the draft horse, with a yawn
Said, "I must stop, I need to yield,
At eight I've got to plow the field."
The crowd it cheered, their love was shown,
And Lucy dropped the microphone.

Lucy pig went home to rest,
Then came some news that was the best;
The rooster crowed outside her pen,
And said that music agent Hen
Wanted to record their songs,
And sell them to the waiting throngs.

Agent Hen she signed them up,
And also, as a follow-up,
She told them they would go on tour,
Around the world they'd play, for sure.
So Lucy packed and said good bye,
To mom and dad, and left the sty.

Rosie's Toesies

Rosie was just ten years old,
And her two feet were always cold.
At school, or playing in the street,
She felt like she had stepped in sleet.

The coldest part of Rosie's feet,
Were her ten toes, and though petite
Her pinky toes were cold as snow,
Which caused her other toes great woe.

"Why" you ask, "were those toes froze?"
I think it was the shoes she chose.

Her parents bought her footwear that
Was sensible, the soles were flat,
The fronts were round, the heels were short,
Inside there was some arch support.

But Rosie liked a fancy shoe,
They could be orange, green or blue,
With little heels and sequins bright,
And pointy fronts that squoze toes tight.

Inside her shoe, her tosies cried,
"Please let us stretch, we're petrified!"
"Especially me!" the pinky gushed,
"I'm bent and pushed and squashed and crushed!"

One day, when walking in the yard,
Her heel sunk in the dirt so hard
That when she tried to move from there,
Her shoe stayed stuck, her foot was bare.

Then Rosie's toes, they touched the grass,
It was so soft, it made her gasp.
With great relief and toes a-thawing,
She could not stop her ooh- and ahw-ing.

From that day on, our Rosie swore,
That never more would she endure
Shoes that hurt her round the clock;
she started wearing Birkenstocks.

Brrrr!

Barns

Do you remember Butterfat,
Who ate and pooped and all of that?
You may have wondered where she goes,
Both when it's dark or when it snows

If the day is bright and clear,
Butterfat will then appear,
And wander to a place preferred,
By all the cows, and meet her herd.

A herd is just a bunch of cows,
That stand in fields and moo and browse,
Sometimes they nap, sometimes they chew,
Sometimes they've cow-y déjà vu.

When it gets cold, or when it's dark,
The cows, each one, they all embark
Along a path and walk aligned,
Or run if they are so inclined.

The cows are smart, they know the way
Back to the barn at end of day,
In the doors, past goats and sheep,
Settle in their stalls to sleep.

The next day when the sun is high,
Or snow has stopped and it is dry,
Our Butterfat will get a yen
To get back to her herd again.

The farmer throws the barn doors wide
So Butterfat can go outside,
And walk the path back to her group,
To eat and moo and doze and poop.

Swimming

In summer, the days are all long and they're warm,
Except when there's thunder and lightning and storm.
On days when it rains most kids stay in the house,
They play games or they sleep, then they moan and they grouse,
They want to go out, to ride bikes or play tag,
To meet with their friends and play Capture the Flag.

On the days when it's hot they might look for a lake,
Or a trip to a river they might undertake,
Maybe a pond where the water is cool,
Or off to the beach or perhaps to the pool.
No matter the setting they're set for a swim,
They want to get wet by the water within.

Some people are bold and they look then they jump
Right into the current they stomp and they flump,
They really don't care if the water is cold,
They're hot and they're sweaty and plop uncontrolled,
While others are timid, they can't just dive in,
They start with a toe and creep in to their chin.

And once they are in they will stay in all day,
They'll swim and they'll splash anyone in their way,
Their fingers will wrinkle, their lips will turn blue,
And they'll only get out when mom calls to the crew:
"You must eat some food from these paper plate dishes,
Or else you might faint and then sleep with the fishes."

Cars

Lucy pig was hoarse from singing,
Her vocal cords and throat were stinging.
She was on tour with Chicken Feather,
The punk-rock band that played together.

Lucy knew she needed help,
Perhaps a lozenge from the shelf
Of a store that sold such tonics,
So she could grunt and snort harmonics.

Lucy got behind the wheel
Inside her bright red pig-mobile.
She clicked her belt, turned on the car,
And started out, it wasn't far.

Lucy's car drove ever nearer,
When just then in her rear-view mirror,
She saw lights flashing, red and blue,
And heard a siren coming through.

She pulled the car up to the curb,
No law she broke, she was perturbed.
She rolled her window down to talk,
To the policeman as he walked.

The cop approached with widened eyes,
And all the shock that that implies.
Never in his life till now,
Did he observe a driving sow.

He strode up to her car and spoke,
"Maam', and this is not a joke,
There's laws against this kind of action,
A driving pig's a code infraction!"

Lucy pig pulled out her purse,
With hopes the scene would not get worse,
She found her license and registration,
And gave them over with some vexation.

The cop he read them, then he said,
"Oh Lucy pig I was misled,
I didn't think a pig could steer,
Or even get a car in gear."

He gave her back her documents,
Apologized, and off he went,
He walked away, then she drove off,
To get some pills to help her cough.

When Lucy reached the parking lot,
She jumped out of the car, and bought
The things to make her voice sound strong,
And pens to write a protest song.

Bed

When someone is young, and their bedtime is near
These are some of the words you might most often hear:
"I don't want to go to bed!"

When someone is old, and their bedtime is near
These are some of the words you might most often hear:
"Is it bedtime yet?"

In any case, whether you're young or you're old,
And whether you choose to lie down or you're told,
You'll go to the room where your bed is within,
Put on your pajamas, or sleep in your skin.

You'll pull down the covers, the blanket and sheets,
Sit down on the edge and then pull up your feets,
You'll stretch out your body, your arms and your back,
Then you'll pull up the covers cause you've hit the sack.

You might toss, you could twist, while you're sleeping, that is,
You might then have a dream about taking a quiz,
You could have a nightmare and wake with a shout,
(On second thought, I think we'll leave this one out.)

And then when the sun rises up in the sky,
A sunbeam may land right on top of your eye,
Or maybe your brother upon you will leap,
Perhaps an alarm clock will rouse you from sleep.

You'll blink and you'll stretch and then up you will stand,
The day is beginning, there's play to be planned,
Except if your brother did force you awake,
And then, oh then, what sweet revenge you will take.

Garages

Our mom has a car and she drives it around,
To take us to practice or school or downtown,
To dentists, to doctors or friends' yards to play,
You'll find her out driving all hours of the day.

We have a garage where the car goes at night,
Our mom steers it in, but the space is so tight,
(There's lots of things stored there, needed or not),
That our mom has one chance to get into the spot.

The garage is the place that we put things away,
In hopes that we might really use them one day.

So...

If you need a shovel or rake or a hoe,
A bucket or mower or rope for a tow,
Some grass seed or peat moss or food for your plants,
Some broken old fencing or traps for your ants.

We have some old toys that would be new to you,
Some tires, a flashlight, a patched-up canoe,
There's nails and a laddder, some tools on a shelf,
Among them sits waiting a Christmas-time elf.

In back's a machine that removes snow and sleet,
Some hoses with holes, and a baby's car seat,
There's paint cans and brushes and rags and some chain,
Three bikes, sixteen cartons, a tiny toy train.

And up overhead there are other things stored,
Our fishing poles, dart set, an ironing board,
A lawn trimmer, wood scraps, two rusty old grates,
Some skis and some poles and an old pair of skates.

The space for the car it is really so small,
It's amazing it even fits in there at all,
Our mom drives it in, then can't open the door,
She sleeps there till morning, then drives us some more.

Spoons

A spoon is a sturdy and helpful utensil.
When you want to eat soup, you cannot use a pencil,
You can't use a fork or a block or a string,
A toothbrush or stick, they would not hold a thing.
Not one can be helpful when trying to sip,
No broth would get up to or inside your lip.

A spoon is just perfect for scooping up juice,
Or eating some cereal, ice cream or mousse.
You take up the spoon, dip it into the bowl,
And then pick up your food with your mouth as the goal.
Once that spoonful's eaten, you'll do a repeat,
And you'll dip it again till there's no more to eat.

The End

Thank you to: Marc Engle for designing and getting this ready for publication, and for being the best husband; Gay Edelman and Project Write Now for support and Open Mic Nights; Fern Wolkin for inspiring the fabric creations; Thea for her overall critiques and copy-editing; and, of course, Aidan.

Title font Grandstander by Tyler Finck at http://www.tylerfinck.com/grandstander/.

CPSIA information can be obtained
at www.ICGtesting.com
Printed in the USA
BVRC100928021221
623088BV00007B/242